HIGH TOP

MY OTHER CAR IS ALSO A
BOX

BROGUE 1

LITTLE TIGER

LONDON

STRIPES PUBLISHING LIMITED

An imprint of the Little Tiger Group

1 Coda Studios, 189 Munster Road, London SW6 6AW • www.littletiger.co.uk

First published in Great Britain 2023 • Text and illustrations © 2023 Little Tiger Press Ltd.

A CIP Catalogue record for this book is available from the British Library

All rights reserved • ISBN: 978-1-78895-572-0

Printed in China • STP/2800/0477/0722

2 4 6 8 10 9 7 5 3 1

HIGH TOP

Tom Lacey

This is **High Top**.

He thinks everything's great,
everything's the best.

He's **fresh out the box**
and **ready to run.**

What? You've never seen a shoe
with a face before?

Comfort KICKS
Comfort KICKS
SNEAKY SNEAKERS
Well Heeled
Hip Hop Flip Flops
Hip Hop Flip Flops
HIGH TOP
HIGH TOP

Well clearly you've never been
to **Shoe Town.**

Welcome.

Back to High Top.
He's the star of this story.

He always
has a
spring
in his
step ...

and
a
smile
on
his
face.

He's
ready
to
dive
straight
in ...

and see
what's
good.

Things
That Are
GOOD

A.N. Author

His laces are loose,

his heel's his caboose.
(Caboose is another word for butt.)

If you need a good giggle
he'll give it a wiggle.

High Top is
Lives-for-Fun
Red.

BUT...

Not for anyshoe.
And that can be a bit of a problem.

WHOOPS!

Lorraine Boot
is playing in
the perfect **puddle**,
she's made for
the water.

*tippy tappy
makes me
happy*

High Top knows
what he's made for,
he's made for **fun**.

And when he sees it, he
dives in...

*feet
first...*

*splishy
splashy*

Lorraine is soaking wet
— on the inside.

(That's the worst.)

But our
fast
friend ...

*too drippy
drippy*

is off again because

SHOE DOWN!

**HIGH TOP
JUST.
CAN'T.
STOP!**

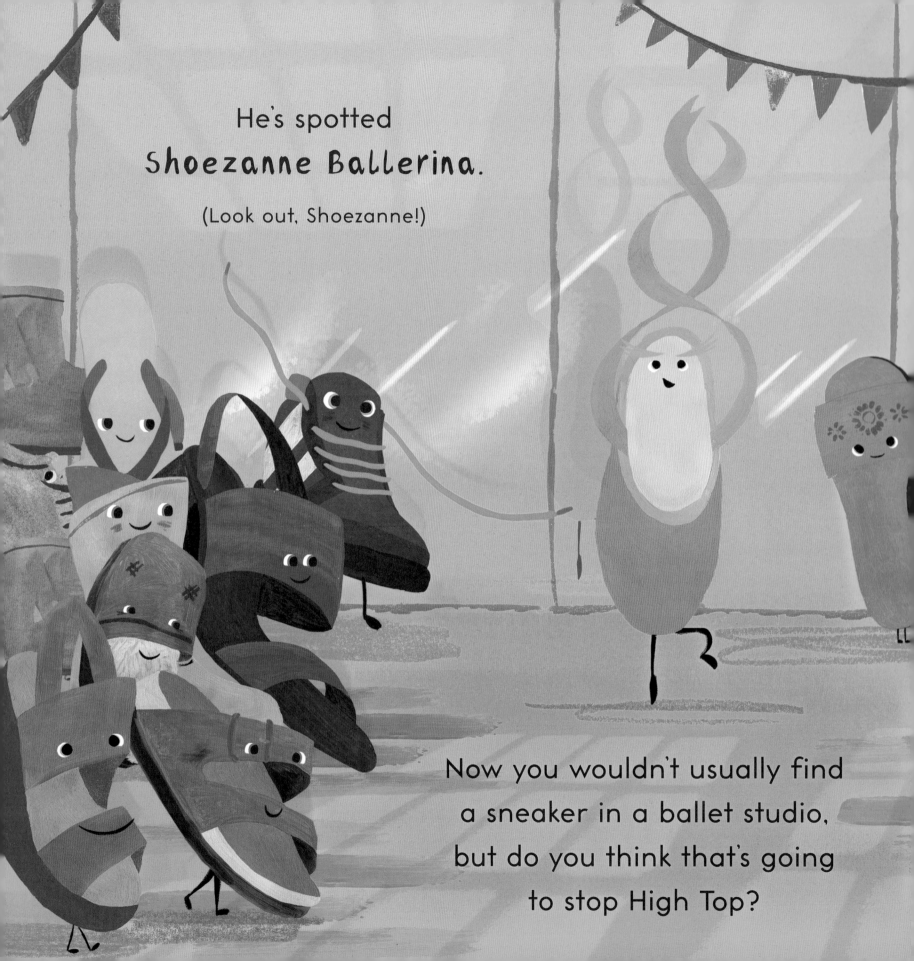

He's spotted
Shoezanne Ballerina.

(Look out, Shoezanne!)

Now you wouldn't usually find
a sneaker in a ballet studio,
but do you think that's going
to stop High Top?

He throws himself into the **dance** ...

sending Shoezanne into a **spin**.

She winds up on her **butt**.

(Caboose for those in the know.)

But does High Top **stop**? Of course not. You know by now

HIGH TOP JUST. CAN'T. STOP!

He's off to visit **Vincent Van Toe**.

Vincent loves to paint.
His favourite colour is sparkly.

Do you think High Top is going to come in and **calmly** look at Vincent's masterpieces?

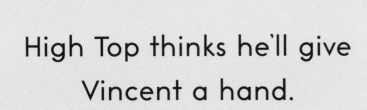

High Top thinks he'll give Vincent a hand.

It definitely needs more **Lives-for-Fun Red.**

OH, HIGH TOP!

But wait a minute. This is unbelievable.
It turns out High Top **CAN** stop.
He's finally worn himself out!

Now this may look like a mouldy old slipper to you, but this is **Platoe**, the wisest footwear you'll ever meet.

(But he is pretty old, I'll give you that.)

Platoe knows how to **relax**. He's had plenty of practice.

He invites High Top to **take a load off.**

"Today I really showed the other shoes how to have **fun**, Platoe."

"Really, High Top? Did **everyone** have fun?"

and Shoezanne ended up in a knot.

Vincent didn't LOVE my help with his masterpiece.

"Oh, Platoe, I just wanted **everyshoe** to have fun. I didn't mean to get **carried away**."

"Sometimes you have to slow down and make sure your **friends** are having fun too."

Do you think High Top knows what he needs to do next?

"I'm sorry, Platoe."

"I know. But it might mean more to your friends if you **can show it**, not just say it."

So High Top **dries off** Lorraine.

(Hairdryer is happy to help.)

He **carefully untangles**
Shoezanne's ribbons.

(And promises she can lead next time.)

And he **helps fix**
Vincent's painting.

(High Top can be
quite creative when
he takes his time.)

But High Top's not done yet. Because as you know...

HIGH TOP

JUST.

CAN'T.

STOP!

The other shoes have come to see what High Top has been doing.

"**There** you are, High Top!"

"**Where** have you been, High Top?"

"**What** have you been up to?"

"Yes, what **have** you been up to?"

"Come and **see!**"